DISCARD

Not in Room 204

Shannon Riggs   Illustrated by Jaime Zollars

ALBERT WHITMAN & COMPANY, MORTON GROVE, ILLINOIS

Dedicated to Rich, Sabrina, Jake, and Carleen, who believe,
as I do, that it's the breaking of silence that is golden.—s.r.

Dedicated to all the teachers who make
a difference every day.—j.z.

Library of Congress Cataloging-in-Publication Data
Riggs, Shannon.
Not in room 204 / written by Shannon Riggs ; illustrated by Jaime Zollars.
p. cm.
Summary: A teacher tells the children in her class to talk to an adult if they are being sexually abused.
ISBN 13: 978-0-8075-5764-8 (hardcover)
[1. Sex crimes—Fiction. 2. Schools—Fiction.] I. Zollars, Jaime, ill. II. Title. III. Title: Not in room two hundred four.
PZ7.R442477Not 2007 [E]—dc22 2006023402

Text copyright © 2007 by Shannon Riggs.
Illustrations copyright © 2007 by Jaime Zollars.
Published in 2007 by Albert Whitman & Company, 6340 Oakton Street, Morton Grove, Illinois 60053-2723.
Published simultaneously in Canada by Fitzhenry & Whiteside, Markham, Ontario.
All rights reserved. No part of this book may be reproduced or transmitted in any form or by any means, electronic
or mechanical, including photocopying, recording, or by any information storage and retrieval system,
without permission in writing from the publisher.
Printed in the United States of America.
10 9 8 7 6 5 4 3 2 1

The design is by Jaime Zollars and Carol Gildar.

For more information about Albert Whitman & Company,
visit our web site at www.albertwhitman.com.

Note

Childhood sexual abuse happens alarmingly often, yet the subject remains taboo. In order to overcome the problem of childhood sexual abuse, we must start talking about it in meaningful ways. An important fact that's often ignored is that the vast majority of childhood sexual abuse is perpetrated *not* by strangers, but by family members and other trusted adults.

All adults must learn to prevent, recognize, and react responsibly to the epidemic of child sexual abuse. Learning about such an incident can be overwhelming, but support is available. For help, contact the ChildHelp USA National Child Abuse Hotline at 1-800-422-4453, your region's child protective services agency, or the local police. Local schools and hospitals can also provide assistance.

Preventing child sexual abuse is an adult's job. It's *your* job. The nonprofit organization Darkness to Light offers a solution—prevention training. Go to www.darkness2light.org and download "7 Steps to Protecting Our Children." Your willingness to help, as Mrs. Salvador does in this story, can make a powerful difference in a child's life.

On the first day of school, Mrs. Salvador said, "At home, when your parents tell you to clean your rooms, you might shove dirty socks under the bed and heap toys in the closet, and you might get away with it."

The children in Room 204 smiled secret smiles.
"But not in Room 204. Here, we keep our desks neat."
Some of the children fidgeted, but Regina Lillian
Hadwig sat up straight.

"In other places, you might get away with less than your best work," Mrs. Salvador said. "But *not* in Room 204."

Jack Galvin and Trevor Jensen smirked.

"In Room 204, if you turn in work that isn't your best, I'll give it right back to you and you'll have to do it over."

Jack whispered, "I think I'll move my desk into the hall."

Mrs. Salvador heard. "Mr. Galvin, you might get away with whispering wisecracks to your neighbor in other classrooms, but *not* in Room 204."

"In other places," she continued, "you might get away with name-calling. You might even call someone 'stupid' or 'dumb.' *Not* in Room 204. In Room 204, *no one* is stupid. I've seen your report cards from last year. I know."

Mrs. Salvador folded her hands neatly behind her back.

In October, in Room 204, Amanda Zadatowski ate Brenda Levitt's Halloween candy without asking.

Mrs. Salvador sent a note home to Amanda's mother.

Dear Mrs. Zadatowski,

Today Amanda ate a chocolate bar that did not belong to her. I have asked her to replace it tomorrow, please.

In Room 204, we do not take what does not belong to us.

Sincerely,
Mrs. Salvador

In November, the class went on a field trip to the aquarium. Just loud enough for everyone to hear, Melanie Dickson said that the tour guide looked like a whale. Regina Lillian Hadwig shook her head with disapproval.

Mrs. Salvador said, "Miss Dickson, children in other classes might get away with making rude remarks, but not the students of Room 204. The students of Room 204 show respect. Please apologize, and then you will be my partner for the rest of the day."

Mrs. Salvador led Melanie to the front of the line.

Report-card conferences were at the end of the term. Regina Lillian Hadwig took a seat beside her mother.

"Regina, I am very pleased with all of your written work. You always do your best. You are a very bright girl," Mrs. Salvador said.

She cocked her head to one side and pursed her lips the way she did when she was grading papers at her desk and thought no one was looking. Regina Lillian Hadwig was always looking.

"Are you quiet at home like you are in school?" Mrs. Salvador asked.

Regina Lillian Hadwig thought of the many ways she kept quiet. Reading. Playing with her Raggedy Ann doll.

There were things her father did that Regina Lillian
Hadwig kept *so* quiet about, not even her mother knew.

"Yes," Regina Lillian Hadwig told Mrs. Salvador.
"I'm quiet at home, too."

Mrs. Salvador nodded. "Maybe this is something
we could work on," she said.

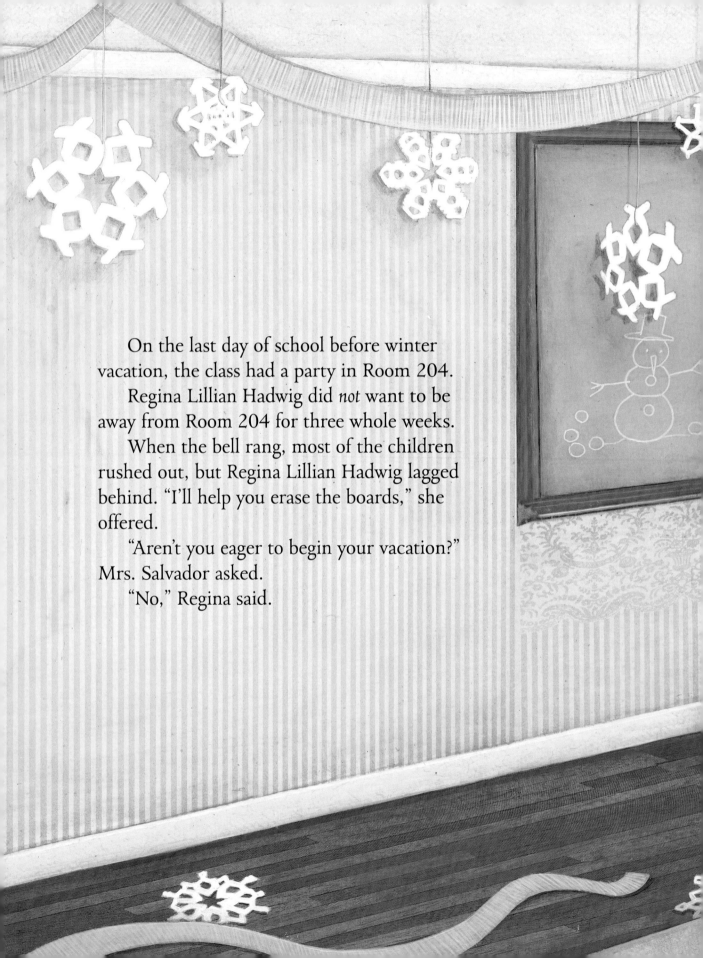

On the last day of school before winter vacation, the class had a party in Room 204.

Regina Lillian Hadwig did *not* want to be away from Room 204 for three whole weeks.

When the bell rang, most of the children rushed out, but Regina Lillian Hadwig lagged behind. "I'll help you erase the boards," she offered.

"Aren't you eager to begin your vacation?" Mrs. Salvador asked.

"No," Regina said.

When all the boards were clean, Regina walked slowly home.

In January, after three days of bitter cold and indoor recess, Jack and Trevor had a fistfight.

Mrs. Salvador pulled them apart and stood between them.
"In Room 204, we keep our bodies to ourselves," she said.
Regina Lillian Hadwig liked the rules of Room 204 very much.

In February, Mrs. Salvador read a book about Stranger Danger, the same lesson they'd had every year since kindergarten. *Don't talk to strangers.* The children in Room 204 slouched in their seats. *Don't get in a car with someone you don't know. A stranger should not touch you anywhere a bathing suit covers.* They'd heard it all before.

A stranger should not touch you anywhere a bathing suit covers.

"I want to talk to you about something else." Mrs. Salvador closed the book. "Knowing about Stranger Danger is important," she said. "But it's not always strangers who touch children in ways they shouldn't be touched. Usually, it's someone the child knows."

The children in Room 204 sat up straight.

"It could be a friend, a babysitter, or someone in your own family. It happens more than most people think." Mrs. Salvador sighed.

Regina Lillian Hadwig felt very small and far away.

Amanda raised her hand. "Has it ever happened to a kid in this school?"

"Yes. More than one."

"Has it ever happened to a kid in *your* class?"

Regina Lillian Hadwig stared at the clock. She watched the second hand click through its slow circle.

"I would never tell other students such a private thing, but I can tell you this. If someone told me this happened to them, I know *exactly* what to do to help."

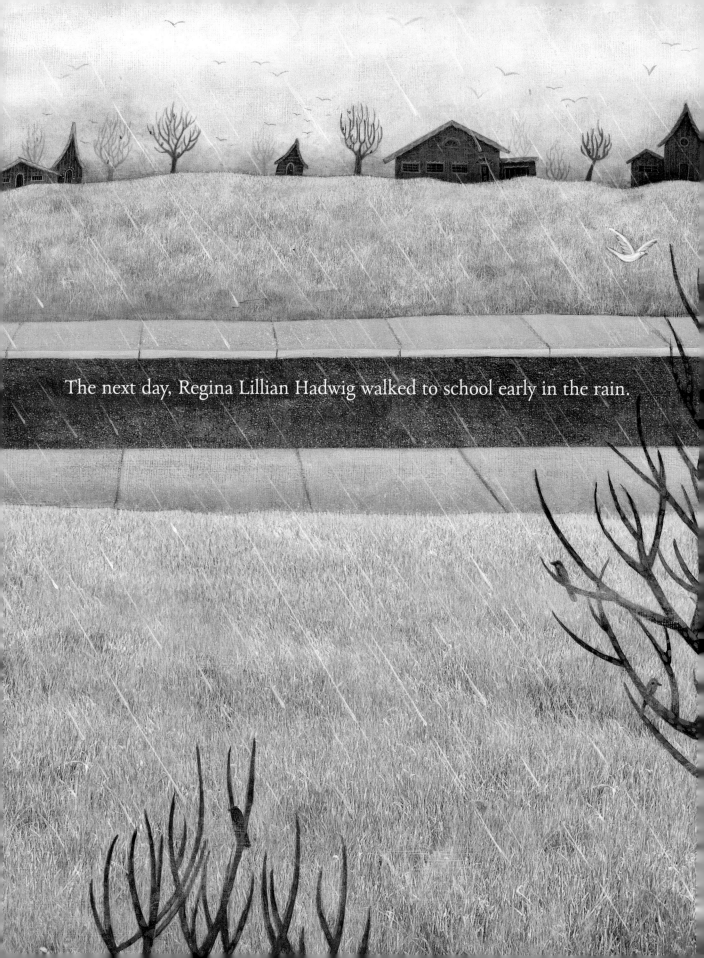

The next day, Regina Lillian Hadwig walked to school early in the rain.

She waited for Mrs. Salvador to make her way from the office to the classroom. Finally, she arrived. She was carrying an overstuffed tote bag, a lunch sack, some mail, a soggy raincoat, and a drippy umbrella.

Regina took a deep breath.

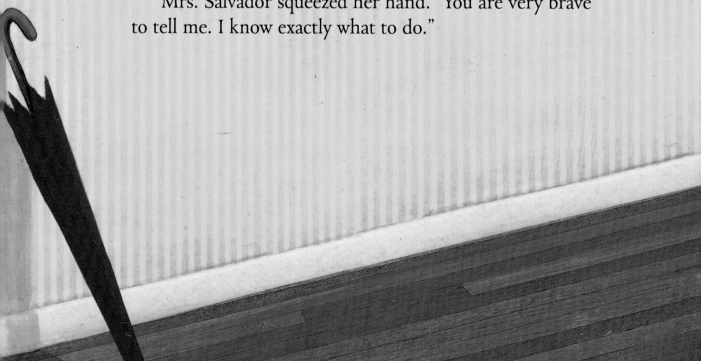

"You're an early bird. Come help me take the chairs down." Mrs. Salvador cocked her head to one side and pursed her lips. "Is there something you want to talk about?"

Quiet Regina Lillian Hadwig's voice sounded small in empty Room 204. "You know how yesterday you said you knew exactly what to do for a kid who—"

"Yes," Mrs. Salvador interrupted. Her brown eyes were kind.

"Do you think you could help *me* like that?"

"Yes. Has someone touched you in ways they shouldn't?"

Regina Lillian Hadwig nodded. She looked away, and then she looked back.

Mrs. Salvador squeezed her hand. "You are very brave to tell me. I know exactly what to do."

Regina Lillian Hadwig looked around Room 204.
Soon the other children would arrive, and a new day
in Room 204 would begin.

"Good," she said. "Let's take down the chairs."

5/07

P9-CRX-169

BOOK SOLD
NO LONGER R.H.P.L.
PROPERTY

CODE ACADEMY

Debugging Disaster!

By Kirsty Holmes

CRABTREE
PUBLISHING COMPANY
WWW.CRABTREEBOOKS.COM

CRABTREE
PUBLISHING COMPANY
WWW.CRABTREEBOOKS.COM

Author:
Kirsty Holmes

Editorial director:
Kathy Middleton

Editors:
John Wood, Crystal Sikkens

Proofreader:
Melissa Boyce

Graphic design:
Danielle Rippengill

Prepress technician:
Margaret Amy Salter

Print coordinator:
Katherine Berti

All images are courtesy of Shutterstock.com, unless otherwise specified. With thanks to Getty Images, Thinkstock Photo and iStockphoto.

Front Cover: Incomible, Nomad_Soul, teinstud, Kamira, Paisit Teeraphatsakool.

Interior: Background: teinstud. Bee – OGdesign. Characters: Ashwin – espies. Bailey – kravik93. Frankie – Kamira. Jia – PR Image Factory. Professor Chip – Elnur. Simon – YuryImaging. Sophia – MillaF. Ro-Bud – Carsten Reisinger. 5 – Iasha. 6 – Bluehousestudio. 9&10 – Grigorita Ko. 10 – doyz86. 12 – ByEmo. 20 – A Aleksii. 23 – By Courtesy of the Naval Surface Warfare Center, Dahlgren, VA., 1988. [Public domain], via Wikimedia Commons.

All facts, statistics, web addresses, and URLs in this book were verified as valid and accurate at time of writing. No responsibility for any changes to external websites or references can be accepted by either the author or publisher.

Some lines of code used in this book have been constructed for comedic purposes, and are not intended to represent working code.

Library and Archives Canada Cataloguing in Publication

Title: Debugging disaster! / Kirsty Holmes.
Names: Holmes, Kirsty, author.
Description: Series statement: Code Academy | Includes index.
Identifiers: Canadiana (print) 2019009883X |
  Canadiana (ebook) 20190098864 |
  ISBN 9780778763390 (softcover) |
  ISBN 9780778763291 (hardcover) |
  ISBN 9781427123374 (HTML)
Subjects: LCSH: Debugging in computer science—Juvenile literature. |
  LCSH: Computer programming— Juvenile literature.
Classification: LCC QA76.9.D43 H65 2019 | DDC j005.1/4—dc23

Library of Congress Cataloging-in-Publication Data

Names: Holmes, Kirsty, author.
Title: Debugging disaster! / Kirsty Holmes.
Description: New York, New York : Crabtree Publishing, [2019] | Series: Code academy | Audience: Ages: 5-7. | Audience: Grades: K-3. | Includes index.
Identifiers: LCCN 2019014221 (print) | LCCN 2019017329 (ebook) |
  ISBN 9781427123374 (Electronic) |
  ISBN 9780778763291 (hardcover) |
  ISBN 9780778763390 (pbk.)
Subjects: LCSH: Computer programming--Juvenile literature. | Debugging in computer science--Juvenile literature.
Classification: LCC QA76.6115 (ebook) | LCC QA76.6115 .H652 2019 (print)
  | DDC 004.2/4--dc23
LC record available at https://lccn.loc.gov/2019014221

Crabtree Publishing Company

www.crabtreebooks.com   1– 800–387–7650
Published by Crabtree Publishing Company in 2020
© 2019 BookLife Publishing Ltd.

All rights reserved. No part of this publication may be reproduced, stored in a retrieval system or be transmitted in any form or by any means, electronic, mechanical, photocopying, recording, or otherwise, without the prior written permission of Crabtree Publishing Company.

Printed in the U.S.A./072019/CG20190501

Published in Canada
Crabtree Publishing
616 Welland Ave.
St. Catharines, Ontario
L2M 5V6

Published in the United States
Crabtree Publishing
PMB 59051
350 Fifth Avenue, 59th Floor
New York, New York 10118

RICHMOND HILL PUBLIC LIBRARY
32972001543893   RV
Debugging disaster!
Sep. 10, 2019

CONTENTS

Hi, I'm Finn and this is Ava. Welcome to the world of coding! In this book you will learn the basics of computers and coding.

After reading this book, join us online at Crabtree Plus to learn about logic, memory, and programming! Just use the Digital Code on page 23 in this book.

Words that are bold, like **this**, can be found in the glossary on page 24.

ATTENDANCE

Code Academy is a school especially for kids who love computers and robots! Time to take attendance! Meet Class 101.

Jia

Bailey

Simon

Frankie

Sophia

Ashwin

Today's lesson is about **debugging code**.
Code is the set of instructions we give to a computer.
Debugging means to find and fix a mistake
in the instructions. The class will find out
the answers to these questions:

- What is a bug?

- What is an algorithm?

- What is debugging?

- Why do you need
  a rubber duck?

Ro-Bud

The students'
robot classmate

Do I hear the bell?

5

MORNING LESSON

This morning, the students at Code Academy are working on their class project. They are writing code to make their **robot** pets move.

Sit!

Ashwins-RoboDog-Fido2.0:$sit=sit

Professor Chip has created robot bees. He is having a problem with the code he wrote to make them fly.

Deactivate! Stop!
Why won't they shut off?
Ro-Bud, help! Start your BeeCatch program!

LUNCHTIME!

Ro-Bud follows Professor Chip's instruction. She runs the program that tells her how to catch all the bees. The bell rings for lunchtime. The class heads to the cafeteria.

Bzzz

Deactivate!

Ro-Bud stays behind because robots do not need to eat. Her job is to feed the class guinea pig, Babbage, every day at lunchtime. Easy, right?

GETTING HELP

After lunch, the students return to the classroom. They notice Babbage does not look very well. Did Ro-Bud feed Babbage the wrong lunch? Guinea pigs are not supposed to eat cheeseburgers!

Oh no! Is there a bug in Ro-Bud's instructions for feeding Babbage?

TO THE WHITEBOARD!

Professor Chip and the students go to the whiteboard. Writing out Ro-Bud's instructions will help them think about the problem.

There must be a mistake in Ro-Bud's instructions for feeding Babbage. Time to do some debugging! Frankie, could you take over while I put the bees away?

DEBUGGING

A computer gets its instructions from a **program**. The set of instructions in a program is called an **algorithm** (say: al-go-rith-um). A computer can only do exactly what the algorithm tells it to do.

Algorithm: Feed Babbage
1. START
2. Open Babbage's Cage
3. Give Food to Babbage
4. Close Babbage's Cage
5. END

FRANKIE FIGURES IT OUT

A mistake in an algorithm can make a computer or robot do things you do not expect.

Put Shoes On

Put Socks On

Walk to School

Shoes before socks? The instructions are in the wrong order!

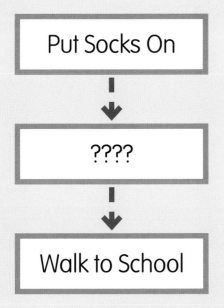

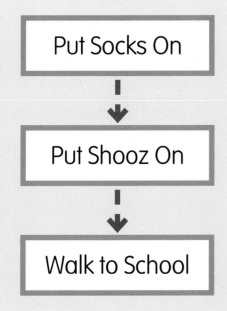

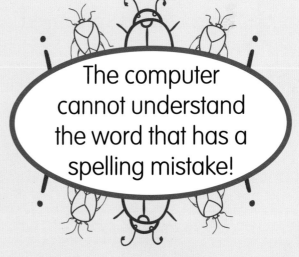

There must be a mistake in the algorithm if a computer does something you do not expect. Mistakes are called bugs. Even a small mistake can make a computer do the wrong thing.

Frankie's Fact:

It's OK to make mistakes. Everyone does!

It's our job to find the bug in the algorithm and fix it. That is debugging! Take a look at this algorithm for brushing your teeth. All the steps are here, but there are three mistakes.

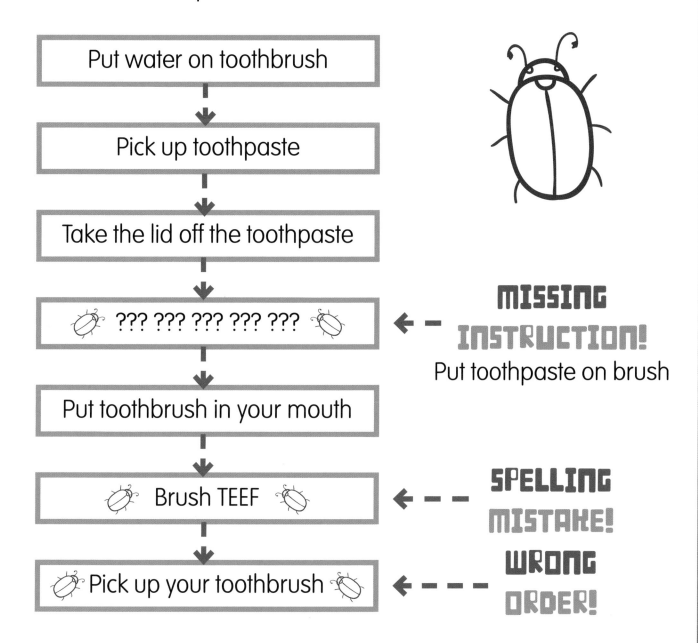

Put water on toothbrush

Pick up toothpaste

Take the lid off the toothpaste

??? ??? ??? ??? ???

MISSING INSTRUCTION!
Put toothpaste on brush

Put toothbrush in your mouth

Brush TEEF

SPELLING MISTAKE!

WRONG ORDER!

Pick up your toothbrush

DEBUGGING SAVES THE DAY!

Now let's take a look at Ro-Bud's program. Why did she feed Babbage a cheeseburger? We need to look at the algorithm one instruction at a time. The first instruction is "START." This instruction is telling the program to begin **running**. That instruction looks right.

1. START

Ro-Bud definitely needs to open the cage so she can feed Babbage. The second instruction says exactly what we want Ro-Bud to do.
This instruction looks okay. No bugs here.

2. Open Babbage's Cage

Suddenly Frankie says, "Wait! I forgot to use the rubber duck!" The rest of the class looks puzzled.

Frankie's Fact:

A good way to help you find a bug is to read the instructions out loud. It can make it easier to spot a mistake. Frankie likes to read to a rubber duck. She listens to each instruction to see if it would make sense to someone who does not know anything about code.

Read the algorithm out loud to me. Explain what each line is asking Ro-Bud to do. This will make it easier to see why Ro-Bud gave Babbage the wrong food!

1. START

2. Open Babbage's Cage

3. Give Food to Babbage

4. Close Babbage's Cage

5. END

Let's see. Instruction number 3 tells Ro-Bud to feed Babbage, but not WHAT food to feed him! It does not give her enough information. I found the bug!

SORTED OUT

Frankie fixes the bug. Now Ro-Bud knows exactly what to feed Babbage. No more bugs here!

Except the flying kind. Shoo! Shoo!

1. START
2. Open Babbage's Cage
3. Give GUINEA PIG FOOD to Babbage
4. Close Babbage's Cage
5. END

A REAL BUG

When computers were first **invented**, a computer once stopped working because there was a moth inside it.

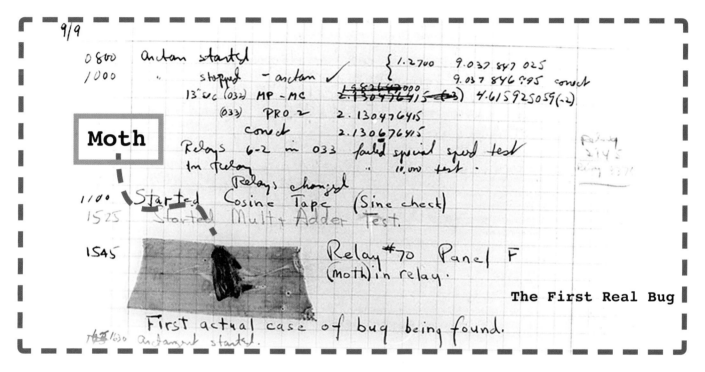

The First Real Bug

Moth

We call a mistake in an algorithm a bug because of that moth!

For fun activities, enter the code at the Crabtree Plus website below.

www.crabtreeplus.com/codeacademy

Your code is:
ca542

LOOK IT UP

GLOSSARY:

algorithm	A set of instructions in a program that tells a computer what to do
code	A set of instructions to a computer
deactivate	To switch something off
debugging	To find and fix mistakes in an algorithm
invented	Made for the first time
program	A set of instructions given to a computer
robot	A machine that performs actions by following instructions in a program
running	When a computer carries out its instructions

INDEX: